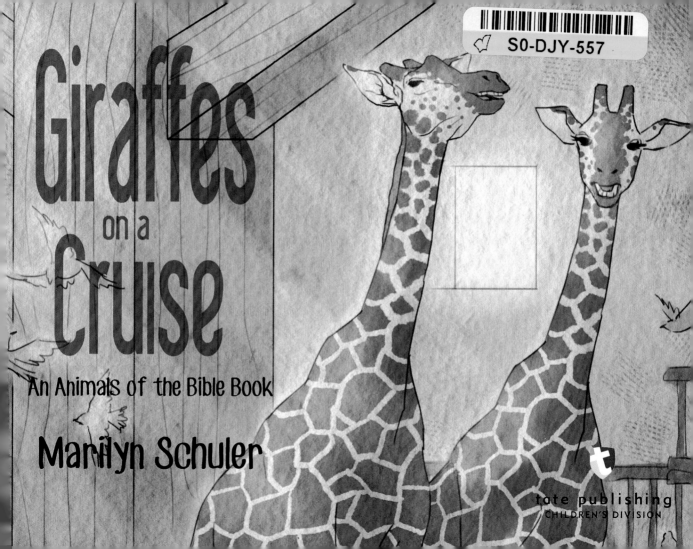

Giraffes
on a
Cruise

An Animals of the Bible Book

Marilyn Schuler

tate publishing
CHILDREN'S DIVISION

Published by Tate Publishing & Enterprises, LLC
127 E. Trade Center Terrace | Mustang, Oklahoma 73064 USA
1.888.361.9473 | www.tatepublishing.com

Tate Publishing is committed to excellence in the publishing industry. The company reflects the philosophy established by the founders, based on Psalm 68:11,
"The Lord gave the word and great was the company of those who published it."

Book design copyright © 2013 by Tate Publishing, LLC. All rights reserved.
Cover and interior design by Errol Villamante
Illustrations by Paul Vasquez

Published in the United States of America

ISBN: 978-1-62902-885-9
1. Juvenile Fiction / Religious / Christian / Historical
2. Juvenile Fiction / Animals / General
13.09.23

Dedication

To granddaughter Sarah, who is fond of giraffes, and to all people who enjoy the animals God created for us.

{ Then the LORD God said, "It is not good for the man to be alone…So the LORD God formed from the ground all the wild animals and all the birds of the sky. He brought them to the man to see what he would call them, and the man chose a name for each one. He gave names to all the livestock, all the animals of the sky, and all the wild animals. }

—*Genesis 2:18–20*. NLT

Jared saw Pace among the giraffes drinking at the river. He walked to her thinking, *I like her because she is fun loving.*

"I want to show you something," Jared said. "Will you come with me?"

They ran to the top of a hill. "Pace, look down in the valley." They heard men shouting.

"What are they doing?" Pace asked.

"I'm not sure," Jared replied. "Our Creator told me to go to the man in the valley when the time is right. I don't want to go alone. Will you go with me?"

Pace hesitated. *Jared is trustworthy*, she thought. "Yes, I'll go with you, Jared. When do we go?"

"Soon I think," Jared replied. "The Creator will tell me."

Every day Jared and Pace went to the top of the hill to watch the people. One morning Jared said, "It is time to go." They walked into the valley and saw many other pairs of animals.

"Welcome," shouted a man standing by a ramp leading into the building. "Enter into the ark of Jehovah." Their turn came to walk into the large doorway and up two ramps.

There was a nice breeze blowing through the opening just below the roof. The giraffes heard voices.

"All the animals are in, Father." Just then there was a rumbling noise.

"The big door is closing," father said. "Jehovah God is shutting us in. Our voyage is beginning."

The giraffes heard something hitting the roof above them. "Pace, try to get your head through this opening," Jared said. Pace stuck her head out. Water was pouring from the darkening sky. Water was running like a river down the valley, starting to shake the building.

"I'm all wet," Pace cried. "I don't like water on my head, and I'm scared! Water has never come from the sky before. There is water everywhere not just in the river!"

"I'm scared too, Pace, but it is dry in here. That must be why our Creator sent us. I trust He has a plan to keep us safe. We will get through this together."

"I don't like any of this," Pace said, "but we have to trust someone."

Weeks passed and the rain continued. Pace would stick her head out and tell Jared, "The mountains are getting smaller!" One day she said, "Jared, the mountains are gone! I only see water everywhere; but the sun is shining, the wind is blowing, and water has stopped falling on my head. I want to go outside."

"I think we should wait until you can see land," Jared replied.

"But it has been so long," Pace complained. "We barely have room to turn around, our neighbors are noisy, and I'm tired of dry grass."

"Now you have sunshine to go with your dry grass," Jared joked.

As the weeks passed into months, the giraffes grew accustomed to the routine. A man came every morning bringing fresh buckets of water and dry grass. "We have an endless supply of water," he laughed, "but not as much hay. Come on, you two, it is your exercise time. You walk the aisle, and I'll clean your stall."

"Come, Pace, a walk will do us good."

"I want to run on the plains," Pace said.

"Someday we'll run with sun on our backs and eat green leaves."

"You're a good friend, Jared, even when I'm grumpy. I'm glad we're here together."

As the giraffes returned from their walk Pace said, "I'm hungry. Are we getting less grass to eat?"

"Pace, look!" Their neighbor's trunk was just retreating back over the partition with a bunch of dry grass. They watched the trunk reach across for more grass. Pace lunged, her teeth coming down hard on the tip of the elephant's trunk. The elephant squealed and pulled his trunk back.

"You are so brave." Jared nuzzled Pace approvingly.

The day finally came when the old man let a raven fly off to look for dry land. When the raven returned the man said, "There is still too much water." The next week the man let a dove fly from the ark. On her second try, she returned with a fresh olive leaf in her beak. She didn't return from her third flight. "It won't be much longer," the man said. "The dove found a resting place."

Weeks later Pace asked, "What is that rumbling noise?

"I think it is the big door opening," Jared said. "Quick, look and see!"

"You are right, Jared. The humans are out on dry ground. Pairs of animals are leaving. Let's go too. "

Jared and Pace paused in the doorway. A multi-colored, striped arch appeared in the sky. Jared whispered, "A sign from the Creator."

"Come, let's find some green leaves!"

—*Genesis 6:9 to Genesis 9:17*

e|LIVE

listen|imagine|view|experience

AUDIO BOOK DOWNLOAD INCLUDED WITH THIS BOOK!

In your hands you hold a complete digital entertainment package. In addition to the paper version, you receive a free download of the audio version of this book. Simply use the code listed below when visiting our website. Once downloaded to your computer, you can listen to the book through your computer's speakers, burn it to an audio CD or save the file to your portable music device (such as Apple's popular iPod) and listen on the go!

How to get your free audio book digital download:

1. Visit www.tatepublishing.com and click on the e|LIVE logo on the home page.
2. Enter the following coupon code:
   1e53-2423-c90e-0506-31a0-a931-853d-9933
3. Download the audio book from your e|LIVE digital locker and begin enjoying your new digital entertainment package today!